SCHMITTY THE WEATHER DOG

Daydream

Written by **Elly McGuire**
Illustrated by **Simon Estrada**

New Yorkie Press
New York

Being a small dog living in a big city can be ruff! Don't get me wrong. New York City is the greatest city in the world. I live way up high in a really cool building, I play in Central Park, and I go for fun walks around the city with my two-legged folks.

But just once I would love to not worry about baby strollers running over me or big feet stepping on me. And don't get me started on high heels. Ouch!

Maybe that's why I daydream so much.
Sometimes I wonder what it would be
like to be really tall, or have bright spots,
or be super smart.

Have you ever wished you were different?

One day my two-legged dad must have been daydreaming about his life too. Since he liked The Weather Channel, he decided to go back to school to become a meteorologist. That's a fancy name for weatherman.

That wasn't easy to do. My two-legged dad was the oldest kid in his class. I'm sure he wished his back didn't ache sitting in those hard, wooden school chairs.

While I was daydreaming, my two-legged dad was taking action. He's my hero.

Every day I watched him
study charts and graphs
to help him predict the
day's weather. But, like most
TV weather humans, he never
seemed to get it quite right.

On rainy days our doorman would laugh when I'd walk into my building. I guess a dripping wet five pound pooch is a pretty funny sight. Or was it because my two-legged weatherman dad didn't bring an umbrella?

One day I woke up from a delicious doggie dream about the weather. Or was it because The Weather Channel was on TV? Whatever. But it got me thinking. Since dogs have such a keen sense of sight and smell, maybe I could become a weather dog and help my two-legged dad.

I visited my two-legged grampa and told him about my idea. He looked down from his duck carvings and said, "You are the best granddog ever, so why would you want to go and do something silly like that?"

I told our doorman, Ralph, too.
He smiled, bent down and patted
me on the top of my head and said,
"Schmitty, you're such a sweet pup . . .
but dogs can't predict the weather."

I even confided in my dog friends in Central Park about my dream to become a weather dog. It took them a few minutes to stop howling before they said that only humans could go on TV and forecast the weather. Why couldn't I just behave like a regular dog?

At first I was hurt and discouraged. Then I thought, "Isn't this America, where anyone, no matter who they are, be it basset hound, border collie, or beagle, can make their dreams come true?" That's when I decided to take action and prove them all wrong.

After everyone left for work, I'd sneak up to the roof deck and lie on my back to watch the clouds go by. With lots of patience, I learned that each cloud gave a clue to the weather. Even my bug and bird friends did things a certain way when a change in the weather was coming.

Hour after hour I would sit by the window sniffing the air, learning what it smells like just before a rainstorm, or a snowstorm, or a thunderstorm.

It wasn't long before I was patiently sitting at the door dressed in my yellow slicker or sunglasses waiting to go out. Something was different about me, but no one could quite put their paw on just what it was. But I knew and now I was ready to help rescue my two–legged dad.

One night when everyone was asleep, I switched on the computer and emailed the top dog at a big TV station in town. I told him I was Schmitty, part of a unique weather team, and would he like to meet us?

The next day I sat by the computer waiting.
Suddenly the computer barked, "You've got mail!"
To my surprise, Mr. Very Important TV Guy emailed
to say that he could meet us the next day. Wow!
My tail started wagging like a windshield wiper.

The next morning my two-legged dad woke up and found the email. Boy, did he look surprised! He couldn't figure out for all the dog biscuits on the planet how this happened. But I knew he wasn't going to miss this big chance.

My two-legged dad took a shower, had his hair cut, and his suit pressed. I had a bath, a trim, and my nails clipped. He grabbed his charts and off we went.

Taxi!

When we arrived at the TV station, a very nice lady told us to sit. After what seemed like forever, she led us into the studio where we met Mr. Very Important TV Guy. He asked my two-legged dad to stand in front of a weather map and talk about the weather.

My two-legged dad looked great. Even his speckled gray hair made him look really smart. But I could tell he was nervous. He wasn't panting, but he was growing little beads of water on his forehead like humans sometimes do.

The bright lights came on, the camera crew was ready, and a small crowd gathered as my two-legged dad summoned up all his courage to forecast the weather . . . and froze! All the humans, including Mr. Very Important TV Guy, were waiting, but nothing happened.

Luckily, I had checked out the cloud formations, smelled the thickness in the air and sensed a rain shower ready to burst. Just in case, I'd brought along my favorite raincoat and rain hat. I quickly slipped them on and to everyone's surprise, jumped up on the desk and sat there in all my yellowness.

At first, my two-legged dad was startled. Then he smiled, pointed to me and blurted out, "I see by her bright yellow rain gear that Schmitty The Weather Dog says it's going to rain this afternoon."

Every human in the room looked at my two-legged dad and then at me. You could hear a dog bone drop. Then everyone turned around and looked at Mr. Very Important TV Guy, who was just staring at us.

Then he started to smile. Then he laughed. He laughed and laughed. Then all the other humans in the room laughed too.

Mr. Very Important TV Guy said, "That was great. That was really great." Then he added, "I'm tired of TV weather being so boring. My viewers deserve better." He thought for a minute and said, "You're hired . . . both of you!"

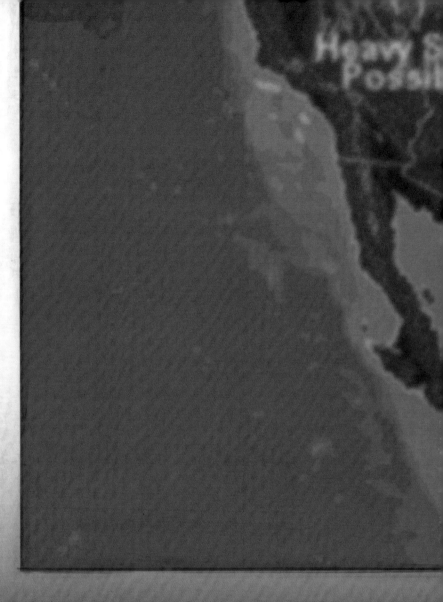

My two-legged dad was more excited than a puppy in a butcher shop. I was so excited I could've just peed . . . but I didn't. Instead, I rolled over, did a little dance, and high fived everyone.

As we walked out the door of the TV station, my two-legged dad looked at me in my bright yellow raincoat and said, "You're my hero!" Then it started to rain.

For Jerry and Pat
Your long distance love and inspiration is why this book exists.
E.M.

To my family, who gave me the courage to follow my dreams.
S.E.

A special thank you to:
Adrianne, Annette Baesel, Karen Kershaw Barnard, Ann Benjamin, Bridget Best, Chuck Bessant, Charlie Blum, Tom Bonanno, Janet Bretz, Jessica Cohen, Terri Cude, Diane DeLuca, Frances Dolan, Michael Edelstein, Robert Erlick, David & Penny Gardiner, Dr. Margie Garret, Gray-Haired Granny, Francine Haas, James Harrison, Marie Harvath, Cara Kenefick, Pat Kidder, John & Jan Kosta, Pam Leibowitz, Lesley Maple. Bradley Maurer, Eileen & Ed McLellan, Mace Michaels, John Monteleone, Cynthia Mooi, Karen Morse, Charlotte Oien, Lorette Phillips, Jared Polis, Buzzy Porter, Esteban Richer, Michal Rosenn, Snowball, Sonya Starr, Iris Spellings, Kathleen Stalker, Yancey Strickler, Margo Ann Sullivan, Nicholas Trotta, Ron Trotta, Loulie Walker, Rita Wilds

Printed in the United States of America

First Edition 2013

ISBN 978-0-9898158-0-2

New Yorkie Press
27 W 67th Street, Suite 5RE
New York, New York 10023

www.NewYorkiePress.com

Illustrations by Simon Estrada

Front Cover Design by James Adamé

Schmitty The Weather Dog's Fashions by New Yorkie®
www.NewYorkieStore.com